RESET

DR. MIDNIGHT

RESET

ISBN 978-0-9825511-9-6

Published by Viscus Vir Publishing

RESET

It's 6:30 a.m. on a Fall morning. Jonas wakes up and goes to brush his teeth. Next, he heads to the kitchen to see his mom. "Mom, did you make breakfast yet?" Jonas asks as he enters the kitchen.

"Don't worry sweetie. Breakfast will be coming soon," says his mom. She starts to search for pots and pans. Her long black hair sways from side to side as she pokes around in the kitchen cabinets.

Jonas smirks. "I'm gonna take a jog."

Jonas puts on his headphones as he prepares to take a jog around the block. Jonas heads towards the neighborhood. It's a pretty standard middle-class neighborhood. All the houses look the same. As Jonas is jogging, he accidentally bangs into a girl that is doing the same thing he is doing. She has her headphones on and is jogging. She is pretty, with black hair and blue eyes.

"I'm so sorry, are you okay?" asks Jonas.

"Oh yeah – I'm fine," she replies.

They look at each other for a solid seven seconds. It is quiet but they both feel something is in the air. They give each other a smile and both go back to what they were doing. All of a sudden, they stop their run and turn back and look at each other. They do this at the exact same time. Realizing this, Jonas quickly resumes his jog. He heads back to his house. When Jonas arrives, he sees that his mother has made him an omelet. He sits down and eats his eggs. He is looking blankly and thinking about the girl he met.

"Jonas are you alright?" his mom asks.

"Yeah mom, I'm fine," he says. Jonas takes a big bite out of his omelet, finishing his breakfast in one mouthful.

Jonas and his mom go to watch some T.V. As he is switching through the channels, Jonas finds a political rally. It shows a man talking about the world, and how things are going now. The man is in his fifties. He has all-white hair. Behind him is a sign that says "Nolan Knows." He talks about how we are all on our own in this world. He is saying that God does not exist.

The man says, "businesses are getting bigger. Companies are getting bigger. I am so glad to be in this world to make money and help other people out. I am going to do something God would not do. I think there are too many beliefs in the world. We all need to forget about Gods and religion. It's all about people. We are our own superpower. I am going to have my own superpower. I will do things that no God will ever do. I will be better than any God. I want all you people to follow me and I will lead you to greatness! If you bless me, I'll bless you. So, let's bless America."

All the people in the rally are shocked. No religious leader in history has ever said these words the way he has, never mind a political figure. Jonas and his mother just stare at the screen.

"I can't believe a guy like him would even say that on T.V. What is he trying to be? He is just a person," Jonas's mom says.

Jonas just shrugs his shoulders and says, "I know."

Later that night, Jonas is lying in bed. He is thinking about what Nolan said. He is restless. He says to himself, "there is something about this guy. I don't know what it is." He falls asleep thinking about what he saw on television.

Jonas begins to dream. He sees Nolan holding this big globe in his hands, and it is a raging inferno. His face has an evil smile. He is laughing. In his mind, Nolan is saying "I got what I wanted. I did it. I finally corrected the world the way it should have been this whole time!"

The next morning, Jonas wakes up and decides to take another jog. He sees the same girl again. This time after he stares at her he says, "hey, did you see that guy on T.V. yesterday?"

"Yeah, he is pretty weird. I don't know why anyone would want to be like that," she replies.

Jonas nods his head and says, "yeah, so what's your name?"

"I'm Martha," she replies.

"Oh cool, I'm Jonas. Really nice to meet you."

She smiles. Then she looks into his brown eyes and says, "nice to meet you too."

"Do you have a phone number?" Jonas nervously asks.

Martha just laughs and says "yeah sure. I'll give you my number."

An awkward silence fills the air. Not knowing how to fill it, Jonas and Martha just walk away from each other. Martha never gives him the phone number.

All of a sudden Jonas stops walking. He turns back towards Martha and says, "be careful."

Martha stops and turns around. She slowly and cautiously says "Okay." Then she continues walking away from him.

Jonas jogs back to his house for breakfast. Jonas is now at home eating his omelet. His mother asks, "are you okay?"

"Yeah mom. I'm okay. Hey mom, I think it's weird some random guy would go on T.V. yesterday and say those things to people. I don't know what would give Nolan the right to do something like that ... honestly."

"People are people Jonas. People sometimes don't know what they are talking about," his mother replies.

Jonas looks at his mother, bewildered. Jonas thinks in his head, "I know exactly what that man was doing and what he said. This man is pure evil and wants to be a world dominator beyond any kind of dominator known to mankind. He knows what he is talking about."

Later that night, Jonas is lying in his bed. He is thinking about the girl he met. As that thought is in his head, he subconsciously begins to dream about Martha. The dream is arousing. He wakes up in a sweat.

The next morning, Jonas goes into the living room where his mother is watching T.V. He sees his mom in shock as she looks at the screen. She is paralyzed with fear. He looks at the T.V. and sees the news. There is chaos going on all over the world. People are violent, and going out of control.

Jonas hears noises coming from outside. He goes over to the window to get a look at what is happening. Jonas looks outside his own window and sees people going crazy. They are arguing and screaming at each other in the streets. Some begin to fight to the death. He runs to his mother and yells, "mom, what's going on?"

His mother just looks at him. Her eyes are filled one hundred percent with horror. She stands up. She speeds to the kitchen. All of a sudden, she picks up a kitchen knife and tries to commit suicide. Jonas is shocked beyond belief.

"Mom what are you doing?" Jonas says as he tries to stop his mother.

She looks at Jonas and screams. The next thing he knows, his mother plunges the knife into herself and she is gone. Jonas is in shock as he screams, "MOM! "

Jonas's eyes fill with tears. His heart fills with rage at the man who started all this. Jonas slowly removes the knife his mother used to kill herself with. Jonas takes the knife, then runs to grab her keys. Next, he goes outside to take his mother's car. His first thoughts are on Martha. He drives away past the crowds of screaming, fighting people.

Jonas drives through the neighborhood hoping to find Martha. He sees her on the ground. She is crying. He rolls down the window and shouts, "Martha get in the car."

Martha doesn't move. She is paralyzed with confusion. Jonas gets out of the car. He grabs Martha, and puts her in the car. He slams his foot on the gas and speeds out of his town. He drives down the highway for hours. As night falls, Jonas starts looking for food and supplies. It's getting late. They park on the side of the road to rest.

"Are you okay Martha?" Jonas asks.

Martha just sits there and says nothing. She quickly falls asleep. Jonas falls asleep at the same time. They wake up the next morning. Each has nothing to say. They hit the road and keep going. They see a convenience store.

"Do you think anyone is in there?" asks Martha.

"Yes, there is someone in there. We have to be careful and steady. We don't know who's in there," Jonas says.

They slowly park and get out of the car. They speed walk to the back of the store. Jonas is sure to bring the knife he took from his house. They sneak in the back entrance. They see two guys inside. One man with a shotgun, and one man standing as a lookout for other people. They clearly don't want anyone else there. They have resources and don't want other people taking any. They want it for themselves. Jonas knows that these guys are going to kill them on sight. But Jonas and Martha need to eat.

Jonas whispers, "I'm gonna get the guy with the shotgun. You take the guy that's standing beside him." As he says this, his grip tightens on the knife in his hand.

"Okay. I'll try," Martha replies.

Jonas creeps up behind the guy, knife ready. He bolts up to the guy and quickly stabs the man in the neck. As this is happening, Martha is trying to fight the other man. He is too strong for her. Jonas tries to go after the other man. As he tries to stab him, the man grabs the knife and tries to kill Jonas instead. He is pressing the knife to Jonas's neck. Out of the blue, Martha grabs the shotgun and kills the man.

Now that the men are dead, Jonas and Martha begin to eat the food that is there. "Eat what you can while it's here. I don't know how long we can stay here. More people will come and ambush us," warns Jonas.

Martha argues, "it's too risky to leave because we don't know who else is out there. It could be a dead-end for us."

"We really need to think about this Martha," Jonas replies.

Throughout the night, they take turns keeping watch in case anyone breaks in. At 12:02 a.m., as Martha is sleeping, Jonas hears bikes coming down the road. He tells Martha to quickly wake up and get ready. They see a group of six people on bikes wearing masks. The people see the car parked outside. They know someone is in the store.

Suddenly Martha and Jonas hear the group shouting towards the store. "We see you in there. Get the fuck out before we spray you with bullets."

Before the group can say another word, Martha and Jonas open fire. They take out four of the people. The other two people fire back. Unfortunately, Martha gets hit in the right arm by one of the bullets. Jonas, in a rage, takes out the last two people with his shotgun.

Martha is screaming with pain. "It hurts!"

Jonas gets painkillers, tweezers, and gauze from the store. He takes the bullet from Martha's upper arm. He gives her painkillers, and wraps the wound up with gauze. Jonas begins to see how dangerous it is to keep on the move. He is glad that at least now they have more weapons and ammunition.

Martha says, "we have to stay here. We don't know what else is out there."

Jonas just takes a breath. He knows she is right. Jonas and Martha begin to check the bodies. They find even more stuff on them. Phones, grenades, and different personal items. Martha begins to check the phones for information.

"Jonas, I found these different locations on the phone. Maybe we don't have to stay here as long as we thought."

"I think it's a bad idea. If these guys have those locations, other people will find out where they are," Jonas says as he takes the phones and smashes them on the ground. "Martha, we have to stay here for a longer time, now that I think about it."

Jonas and Martha prepare the store to protect it from any more strangers that will show up. They decide to stay at the store till they run out of supplies. Now that they are settled in, Jonas awkwardly asks, "Martha, what happened to your family?"

"My father went insane. He rushed out of his room screaming. He shot my mother with his gun. When he saw what he did, he shot himself." Martha chokes back tears as she tells the story.

"The same thing happened with my mom. She used a knife to kill herself … this knife," Jonas says as he slowly holds up the blade that ended his mother's existence.

Three weeks later, they are both sitting at the front counter of the store. "We are running out of food Martha," Jonas says.

Martha just looks at Jonas with a sad expression. She doesn't want to leave. Jonas continues, "look at all the weapons we have now. We have to get out there."

Martha finally speaks. "I'm scared right now. I don't want to try to get out there. We will die."

"We have to leave Martha. Get all your stuff ready." They get all their supplies and put them in the car. "Keep the guns in the front seat Martha," Jonas adds.

They get into the car and start to drive. They both are sad because the world they knew is gone. Things will never be the same again. As they are driving they see signs that say things like 'The purge has begun', 'Nolan rules', and 'All hail Nolan.' They look at the signs in disappointment.

They continue to drive down the road. They see one big van and two motorcycles coming up behind them. "Look out," Jonas shouts. He sees the two men on the bikes approaching. One has an Uzi machine gun, and the other has a pistol with a silencer on it.

Martha and Jonas get into a gunfight with the men on the motorcycles. Jonas takes out the guy with the silencer. Martha takes out the man with the Uzi.

Now the van is coming up behind them quickly. As the van approaches, the passenger on the right side tries to aim a gun at Jonas. As the passenger lifts his pistol, the van unexpectedly explodes.

Martha and Jonas pull over. They see a group of nine people standing in front of them on the side of the road. Jonas and Martha get out of the car. The group comes near them.

Jonas holds up his hands and says, "hold, wait, wait, wait! We don't want any trouble with you guys. We just want peace."

One of the men pulls out a pistol and shoots Jonas in the knee. Martha screams. The man then shoots Martha in the knee. They are both on the ground in agony.

The leader comes up to Martha and Jonas. He grabs Jonas's hair and pulls his head up. He says, "Who are you?"

Jonas replies, "I'm Jonas."

He then asks Martha. "What about you?" Martha cries her name in agony. The man then says, "I'm Jason. I wasn't sure if I could trust you guys. I could have killed you if I had the urge to."

The group grabs Martha and Jonas. They put them in their van. The strangers clean up the wounds from the gunshot as the van starts to move.

Jonas and Martha are both laying in the van. While they lay in silence, a girl comes up to Jonas. She says hi to him.

"Jason can be a bastard at times. But when you get to know him, he is a nice guy," she says to Jonas. "I'm Kate."

Kate then looks at Martha and says, "hope everything goes okay."

They make it to the group's fortress. It's in the city. It is surrounded by all these skyscrapers. The fortress is in a giant building that Jason's group has raided. The group carries Jonas and Martha into the building. Martha and Jonas see a bunch of other people in the room with them.

Kate makes the introductions. "This is Wyatt. He's good with computers, tech, downloading, and hacking things. Over here is Larry. He keeps a lookout for things for us." Kate points to a big guy looking out the window. "You can stay here with us and recover for as long as you want to," she says smiling.

Jonas is suspicious of all of them. He thinks, "how can they shoot us and now be so nice?"

Next, Kate takes out some medical equipment. Kate removes the bullets from their legs. She again cleans the wounds, and stitches them up. "You'll recover pretty quick, like in a day or so."

Jonas looks at Martha and says, "are you okay?"

"I don't know how I feel right now Jonas," she says as she sighs.

For the rest of the day, Martha and Jonas don't talk. They just sit there and rest. Jonas is resting on a cot in the room. He begins to dream. In the dream, Jason is staring at Martha with a maniacal look on his face. Martha quickly twists her neck to look at him. She begins to scream at the top of her lungs. Jason speed walks toward Martha, planting a gun on her. While looking at Jonas, he shoots Martha and kills her. Jonas wakes up terrified and surprised. He quickly turns to Martha to make sure it was a dream. She is fine.

Kate walks into the room and announces, "rise and shine!"

Jason storms into the room and yells, "wake up morons! This isn't your mom's house."

Jonas and Martha notice that there is food being served. Their only option is canned food heated up by microwave. They all begin to eat breakfast. "It's my homemade recipe," Kate jokes.

Jason yells, "shut up! You don't fucking cook."

Everyone is silent. As the group is eating, they start watching T.V. Out of the blue, Nolan comes on. They realize that Nolan has hacked all the T.V. systems. Nolan begins to speak.

"Hey everyone, you may know me by a lot of things. You may call me a crazy person, the devil, or a monster. I am none of these things. All of you people should be relying on me. I want to help this world be the way it should be. I want to do it, but I can't do it without you guys. If you don't join me, then you will be executed. I will send my people to take care of this. I can do this right now by snapping my fingers."

Jason says, "this idiot thinks he is Thanos." Everyone then begins to laugh.

Nolan continues: "Everybody fight for your religion. Have one belief in the world. Fight for that one belief to overcome all the dishonesty. Have one real religion take over this world. Fight for your religion. Discontinue the false beliefs that are in the way of what we really should be believing in."

Jason turns the T.V. off and says, "I don't believe this fucking bullshit. I know exactly what this guy is doing. He wants everyone on the planet to just kill each other so he can have world domination."

The group can hear the sounds of yelling and screaming outside their window. "Can you hear that now?" asks Jason. "They are doing it now as we speak."

Kate turns the T.V. back on and switches the channel. Everyone stares at the screen as they see the world fighting. The footage is being filmed from a helicopter in the sky. The camera zooms in on a massive battle-ground. It shows a plaza at the center of five streets. Masses of people are marching up all the streets in the direction of the plaza.

Coming up one street is a group of Catholics and other Christian denominations. They carry banners with crosses on them. Priests and bishops can be seen leading this group.

Marching up another street is a group of Satanists. They are dressed in black cloaks. They carry flags, knives, and spears with satanic symbols. Their faces are twisted with rage.

Moving up the next street is a group of Buddhists. They hold flags with pictures of Buddha on them. They are chanting something.

Advancing up the next street is a group of Atheists. They have signs that say 'there is no such thing as God' and 'fuck Satanism'.

Coming up the final street is a group of Jewish people. They have flags with the Star of David. They are carrying swords with Jewish symbols.

The five groups converge at the center. The Buddhists have a microphone. They start by making a speech. They urge the world to stop fighting, and instead embrace peace and harmony. They say that peace is the only solution. Everyone needs to put down their weapons now. Their leader asks "what is the point of all this?"

As the Buddhists talk, the Satanists yell insults from their corner. They tell the Buddhist leader to shut up. One Satanist emerges from the group and shouts "you all will scream before you go to hell with us. Let Lucifer cleanse your soul. Let him recreate you into what you all really are."

The other Satanists make a hissing sound in support of their leader. They sound like a giant snake as they hiss together. The leader says, "join us, build Lucifer's kingdom. Help us grow. Help Lucifer escape the prison God put him in along with all of us in it." The Satanists start performing demonic rituals in the back of the crowd.

Out of the blue a group of Atheists step forward. There are thousands of people behind them. They say, "this is all bullshit, none of this is real."

As the Atheist is talking, one of the Christians says "your minds are too little to know what reality is. All you people are a disgrace to mankind. You think so poorly of the truth." As he speaks he points his finger at the Atheists.

The Christian continues, "this is an outrage. All of us should not be fighting. This is not what God wants. And this is not God's way either. He didn't create us so we can all be killed in the end. This should not be happening to humanity."

The Catholic leader steps in and adds, "how could you think so little about the world? About mankind itself. How come you have such little belief? You think that once you die, it's complete darkness. We don't need people like you in this world."

The Jewish leader comes forward. He looks toward the Christians and Catholics and says, "how could you believe Jesus Christ is the son of God. He was just a talented man who miraculously knew how to help people. Both of you are so pathetic to think Jesus Christ was the son of God. The real Messiah will be born shortly."

The Atheists reply, "why do we need you Jews and Catholics? All you guys are worried about is whether or not you will go into Heaven or Hell. Your beliefs are so negative about mankind itself. It's obscene to have a group of people believe such things. This is why we don't need people like you in this world."

The main Catholic leader then calmly says, "so be it. Shall God have mercy on your soul."

The groups clash and begin their final war. The Catholics are using crosses with knives on the end of them. The Atheists use regular daggers and guns. The Satanists have knives and spears with the Satanic flag on them.

Suddenly, the screen switches to Nolan. As the world is fighting, Nolan tells his men, "I want all of you to go out there and annihilate all these wars that are going on." His men go out from country to country, and kill everyone in sight.

Jason says, "we can't stay here anymore."

Kate says, "why? we are pretty well supported here."

"People are going to come any minute and raid this place," Jason replies. Jason then adds "I want to go outside and have some fun."

Everyone in the fortress knows what Jason means when he says that. Jason opens the door. He sees a whole bunch of people storm the building at the bottom of the stairs. Little does the crowd know that Jason has set up booby traps on the stairs, so he can watch the people perish as they try to reach him. Jason starts shooting blindly, spraying a carpet of bullets into the crowd. He begins to throw grenade after grenade at the people. There are so many people that it doesn't do much to the crowd.

Jason then pulls out an Uzi and begins to spray the crowd. Because it is so chaotic and there are so many people, Jason gets shot by someone in the crowd carrying a pistol. He collapses on the floor covered in blood.

Larry sees this and screams. He is infuri-ated. He doesn't care anymore. He runs down the stairs and begins to punch everyone as hard as he can. Even though he takes out a bunch of people, it is too much for him. He is overtaken by the crowd and gets killed.

Kate shuts the door and locks it. She runs to Jason to check him. Jason grabs Kate by the shirt and says, "don't worry about me, you can't worry about me." He then falls silent.

Kate screams in horror, "no Jason! Jonas, Martha – help, help!"

Jonas says, "he is gone Kate. There is nothing we can do. We need to leave now!"

Kate is so overwhelmed by it all. She has a pistol in her hand. She takes the gun, points it toward her head, and pulls the trigger. Jonas yells, "NO!" He tries to stop her, but it is too late. She falls to the ground, bloody and lifeless.

Jonas and Martha are trapped in the room. Outside the door, there are millions of raving people all fighting and killing each other. No one can make it up the stairs because they are fighting and killing each other along the way. Jonas says, "we just have to wait here Martha, it will be over soon. Everyone will be dead soon. Just sit tight here. We don't have to go any-where at the moment." After a few minutes, he adds, "we need make a plan Martha."

Martha cries. "I can't think of anything Jonas. What are we gonna do?"

"I know what to do. I am going to kill Nolan and put an end to this all," Jonas says in a determined tone.

Martha looks shocked. "How are you gonna do that?" she asks.

"It's predictable. Trust me, Martha. Even Nolan's own soldiers are going to go crazy and kill each other. The only people who will then be left are you, me, and Nolan. We are going to wait here for two hours. Then we will get all our stuff, all our weapons, and go kill Nolan. Just watch," Jonas says confidently.

As the world either fights in the streets or watches T.V., Nolan is in his skyscraper. He is in his control room. Nolan pulls out some kind of map of the whole world from a secret compartment in his desk. There are all these green switches next to it. Each switch stands for a different country. When a switch turns red, it means that the bombs are launched and the country is annihilated. Nolan starts to flick the switches. He decimates whole continents, except the one he is on. All the people in faraway regions are soon gone.

Jonas and Martha are shocked to see continents being destroyed on the news. After a few hours, there are only three people left. Martha cries, "I can't believe this is happening."

Jonas just blankly believes nothing. Nolan has wiped out each country one by one, with each flip of his finger.

Martha then says to Jonas, "what do we do at this point?"

Jonas says, "we have to get rid of this monster. No matter what it takes."

They gather all their weapons and head to take Nolan out. As they are driving toward his fortress, they are shocked to see how the world has been destroyed. It looks like an apocalyptic desert all around them. Nolan's doomsday bombs have flattened the land. They see decomposing bodies spread all over the rubble.

Nolan is out on the top of his skyscraper. He looks out over the world he created and says, "I God … am Nolan almighty. I was meant to be the only being on this planet and have the world all to myself. How come you didn't stop me from the actions I committed? There is no God. I am God. The world is meant to be mine this whole time. There is no one above me. I am above everyone."

Jonas and Martha see the huge skyscraper in the distance. They don't say anything. They have a vengeful, disgusted look on their faces. As they get closer to the tower, Nolan spies them driving up. Nolan grabs his weapon and goes down the elevator.

"We're almost there," Jonas says.

Martha looks over at Jonas. She weighs the thought that this could be their final moments. She says softly, "I love you Jonas."

"We are going to get through this," Jonas says.

Jonas sees that Nolan is now outside his tower. He sees that Nolan has a grenade in his hand. Nolan throws the grenade under their car.

Jonas quickly says, "get out of the car!"

Right as they get out of the car, it explodes from the grenade Nolan tossed at them. All of their weapons are destroyed except for the pistol Jonas has on him.

"All this is going to end right here, right now you Devil!" Jonas screams toward Nolan.

"You are not allowed to talk to me. I did not give you dominion to talk. This world is mine to own. You're nothing in this world. You're just a speck of dust that should have been executed with everyone else. Somehow you are miraculously alive," Nolan screams.

Jonas loudly replies, "shut up! God is the creator of this world. You are just an imposter who is greedy to have the whole world in his hands. You are an abomination who was made in the world God created. Do you really think God would have wanted you to have the whole world to yourself?"

"I am God!" Nolan screams.

Jonas yells out, "nooooo! You are living in some fantasy that is not even real. You are living a lie. Right now, you are only living inside your own twisted mind, thinking your mind and imagination are in reality. That right there is the Devil's workshop."

They both pull out their guns at the same time. Instead of shooting Jonas, Nolan shoots Martha. Jonas fires at Nolan. Jonas's bullet finds its mark. It pierces Nolan's chest. Nolan falls to the ground on his knees. At the same time, Martha cries out in pain, and falls to the ground too.

Jonas runs to Martha. "Martha are you okay?" he asks.

Martha replies, "don't worry Jonas. I'll be okay."

Nolan is on his knees. Jonas speed walks over to him with his gun ready. Nolan reaches for his gun. Jonas quickly shoots Nolan's hand so he can't pick up the gun. Nolan screams in pain. He grabs Nolan by the back of his scalp. "How the fuck could you have done this?" Jonas asks.

"Just think of how annoying the world is. Having billions of parasitic souls that would spread negativity everywhere. Spread false beliefs that would never make sense, and would make the world so irritating. I want all those vapid souls to die a painful death. To burn, to cripple up. Like helpless newborn babies that would evanesce deep through the ground of the earth. Wouldn't you want to get rid of all the worthless, inferior lives in this world? Wouldn't it be good to have the world rest in your hands? To have all of paradise to yourself?" Nolan asks seriously.

"For what reason Nolan? There would be no point in anything if there was just one human being in the world. There would be a point to something if there are more human beings in the world. The world is not owned by you. The world is for everyone. God created it for everyone to live in. To enjoy peace and harmony. You took that away from everyone and everything. Did you get what you wanted? Did you get what you fucking wanted? Killing billions of innocent people, even the people that bowed down and worshipped you. How can you be so evil?" Jonas asks.

Nolan just begins to laugh psychotically and says, "burn like all the other babies. Just like how your pitiful family burned."

Jonas then points the gun to Nolan's head and calmly pulls the trigger. Nolan falls lifelessly flat on his back. Jonas walks over to Martha. She starts crying again. He hugs her.

Jonas says, "we are going to be okay Martha. We are at peace now. It's okay. We can grow a new generation coming from us, that will grow throughout billions of years. This is how the world was made before Martha." They continue to hug each other in the silence of their new Garden of Eden.

www.ingramcontent.com/pod-product-compliance
Lightning Source LLC
Chambersburg PA
CBHW071353130626
46556CB00005B/2163